The Boy from Planet Nowhere

by
Anne Schraff

Perfection Learning® Corporation
Logan, Iowa 51546

Cover Illustration: Doug Knutson
Cover Design: Deborah Lea Bell

For information, contact
Perfection Learning® Corporation
1000 North Second Avenue, P.O. Box 500
Logan, Iowa 51546-1099.
Tel: 1-800-831-4190 • Fax: 1-712-644-2392

Paperback ISBN 0-7891-4927-3
Cover Craft® ISBN 0-7807-8004-3
Printed in the U.S.A.

1

Some of the students at Canyon High School thought Gilberto Aguilar and Lauren Escoto were brother and sister since they lived in the same house. But they were not related, and the middle-aged couple who owned the older, Victorian-style home were not their parents. Gilberto and Lauren were wards of the state, in other words, foster children. The Crocketts had no children of their own, and they had been taking in foster children for more than a dozen years. Gilberto had arrived six months ago when the people who ran the home he had been living in moved to another state. Lauren had joined the Crockett household more than a year ago when her mother said she couldn't handle her anymore.

Shortly after Gilberto had arrived, Lauren asked him how many foster homes he'd been in.

"Ten, maybe twelve," Gilberto replied.

"Man, you must be a real pain," Lauren had said, laughing dryly.

"Not really," Gilberto said. "It's just that every time my mom got me back, she'd mess up, and the state would take me away again. Sometimes my grandmother would take me. She was the only family I had besides my mom. But Gram died a couple of years ago. Anyway, for the most part, I got sent to foster homes."

"Well, this place isn't too bad," Lauren said. "The Crocketts are okay. Just don't mess up because they won't stand for any trouble. You'll be out of here before you can say, 'juvenile delinquent.' "

"Thanks for the warning," Gilberto said. "I'll keep that in mind."

Gilberto had no intention of "messing up." He was seventeen and a half already, and in another six months, he'd be considered an adult. That meant no more foster homes. He had a part-time job at a fast-food restaurant and was saving money to buy a car. On his eighteenth birthday, he planned on taking off like a rocket, hitting the road to anywhere.

Gilberto had no plans for college. What for? he wondered. He was a nobody and had no real dreams. At least he had been told most of his life that he was a nobody by teachers, counselors, even the kids he met at the many schools he'd gone to over the years. Not in so many words, of course, but in their attitude toward him. And so far Gilberto had no proof that they weren't right.

* * *

Gilberto walked into his drama class. It was the beginning of the second semester. He took the usual place he took in classrooms: the desk in the back corner of the room, as far away from the teacher as possible.

Gilberto had taken drama because it was supposed to be an easy course. He had heard that the teacher, Mrs. Durkin, was an elderly woman who was "coasting" until her retirement at the end of the year. She made the kids read a few plays out loud in class and then discuss them, but that was about it. Drama class was supposed to be an easy *C* even if you slept through half the classes.

But as Gilberto took his seat, he noticed a young man of about thirty sitting at the teacher's desk. Must be a substitute, Gilberto thought.

When the bell rang, the man stood up in back of the desk.

"Good morning," he said in a resonant voice. "I'm Mr. Rhineman, and I'll be your drama teacher this semester."

"What happened to Mrs. Durkin?" one student asked.

"Mrs. Durkin has some health problems that were just discovered last month," Mr. Rhineman said. "So she decided to finish out the first semester and then take an early retirement."

A general murmuring went through the class, and sighs of disappointment could be heard. It was obvious the students weren't happy with this new turn of events.

So much for an easy grade, Gilberto thought.

"With the principal's permission, I'll be making some changes in the curriculum," Mr. Rhineman continued. "Our first project will be a play we'll be putting on for the community—*Othello* by Shakespeare. Everyone will be required to participate in some way."

Now the murmurs and sighs turned to audible groans.

"Hold on, hold on," Mr. Rhineman said, raising his hand. "This is, after all, drama class, and my job is to teach you about drama. I firmly believe that the best way to do that is through hands-on experience. As my mother used to say, 'Experience is the best teacher.' "

Gilberto shook his head. The last thing he wanted to do was act in front of an audience. He decided he'd try for a job on the lighting or scenery crew.

Mr. Rhineman came out from behind the desk. As he did, the students noticed that he carried a white cane.

"He's blind!" Gilberto heard Brandy Engberg say to her friend, Ming.

Mr. Rhineman heard her comment. "Yes, I'm blind, for those of you who haven't noticed." He chuckled at his little joke. "But that doesn't make me deaf, you know. By the way, who is the young lady who made the comment?"

Brandy looked around self-consciously. "It was me," she said quietly. "Brandy Engberg."

"You have a very distinctive voice," Mr. Rhineman commented. He switched on the overhead projector on the corner of the desk. "Please read the first line on this transparency, Brandy."

Gilberto looked at the quotes listed in bold type on the transparency. According to the heading, each one was from the play *Othello*.

Brandy read the first line.

My love doth so approve him,

That even his stubbornness, his checks and frowns . . .

Have grace and favor in them.

Mr. Rhineman smiled at her. "Good," he said. "Now, try it again with this in mind. You love the man you're talking about so much that no matter what he does, it pleases you."

Brandy read the line again, this time with more expression.

"Excellent! Very clear, very expressive. Now, class, we're going to go around the room, and everyone's going to read a line from *Othello*. I want to get an idea of what kind of talent I've got here. Please state your name before reading the quote on the overhead."

As each student read, Mr. Rhineman

listened closely. He seemed to be memorizing their voices and connecting them to their names. When it was Gilberto's turn, he read, "How sharper than a serpent's tooth it is to have a thankless child."

"Wonderful," Mr. Rhineman raved. "Gilberto, you have a fine, full-bodied baritone. We may have found our Iago, class."

Quickly Gilberto spoke up. "I'm not an actor," he said.

"Oh, you've tried acting?" Mr. Rhineman asked.

"Well, no, but I've never done anything like that," Gilberto said. "I wouldn't be any good at it."

"At the risk of sounding like my mother again," the teacher said, "you never know until you try."

Just then the bell rang. "See you tomorrow, class," Mr. Rhineman said.

Gilberto didn't agree with what Mr. Rhineman had said. He could never see himself in front of an audience. He didn't have to try acting to know he wouldn't like it.

After class, Gilberto ran into Lauren

coming from her computer class. "Boy, that was a short class," Lauren said. "It seemed like we hardly got started when the bell rang."

"Wish my morning had started out that well," Gilberto said. "We've got a new teacher for drama. Mrs. Durkin took early retirement. This new guy's blind."

"Blind?" Lauren asked. "How does a blind guy teach?"

"I guess I'll find out," Gilberto said. "He says we're going to put on *Othello* by Shakespeare. He told me I might be some guy named Iago."

Lauren laughed. "Somehow I can't see you on stage," she said. "You're so shy. Even Mrs. Crockett says so."

"What else does Mrs. Crockett say?" Gilberto said.

"Nothing. Just that you must have some kind of psychological problems that make you so shy," Lauren answered. "She didn't tell me that. I just overheard her and Mr. Crockett talking to your caseworker. See you later, Gil." She walked off down the hall.

Gilberto was somewhat miffed as he

headed toward his next class. He resented Mrs. Crockett's remark. What right did she have saying things like that? She hardly knew him. And evidently Mr. Crockett agreed with her. Gilberto had never really bonded with any of his foster parents over the years. It looked like the Crocketts were going to be no exception.

Then again, Gilberto couldn't really argue with the Crocketts' attitude. He often felt weird and stupid himself. He never knew what to say to people, and when he did say something, it was often the wrong thing. He wasn't surprised that other people thought he had problems.

Later at lunch, Gilberto sat at a table not too far from Brandy and Ming. The girls didn't seem to notice he was there. Gilberto was used to that. Once people figured out he was a nobody, they ignored him. All his life, Gilberto felt he had been one of the kids from "Planet Nowhere." He had once heard a counselor use this term. These were the kids who seemed to get through the public school system without being noticed. They were slightly below-average students, usually pulling

C minuses and *Ds*. But they didn't fail their classes, so they didn't present any real problems for the teachers. And because the teachers didn't notice them, the other students didn't either. "Came from nowhere, going nowhere," the counselor had said.

Now Gilberto heard Brandy and Ming discussing him as if he weren't there.

"I'm going to try out for the part of Desdemona," Brandy was saying. "After all, Mr. Rhineman said I had a great voice."

"He was just kidding," Ming replied, chuckling. "I mean, for crying out loud, he said Gilberto could be Iago!"

Both girls burst into laughter. "You know, though," Brandy had said once she recovered, "Gilberto does have a nice voice. I never really noticed it before."

"Yeah, but he turns bright red whenever he has to speak in class," Ming said. "You remember him in government class last semester, don't you?"

The girls laughed again. "He lives in a foster home, doesn't he?" Brandy asked. Ming nodded as she took a bite of her macaroni and cheese.

"Who gets put in those places anyway?" Brandy went on.

"Kids whose parents don't want them or can't handle them," Ming said. "Sometimes the parents are druggies; sometimes they're abusive."

"I'd hate to live with someone who wasn't part of my family," Brandy said.

"Yeah, it can probably mess up the kid even more," Ming agreed.

The girls finished their lunch and carried the trays to the conveyor belt. Gilberto watched them go as he finished the sandwich Mrs. Crockett had made him that morning. He shook his head. Ming's remarks about foster kids hadn't been far off. Gilberto's own mother had been on drugs when he was born. For years she had tried to break the habit but never quite succeeded. Finally, when Gilberto was seven years old, she had died of an overdose.

Gilberto had mixed feelings about his mother's death. He was sad, of course, that she had died. When she wasn't on drugs, he remembered his mother as being kind and loving. But if she was going to die anyway, he sometimes wished she had died when he was a baby. He felt guilty about this feeling, but he couldn't help it. If his mother had died when he was an infant, he might have been adopted by a real family. By the time death finally ended his mother's parental rights for good, Gilberto was a big-for-his-age, seven-year-old introvert. Anyone who was interested in adoption was reluctant to look seriously at a child like Gilberto.

Gilberto picked up his sack lunch and went outside. As he was finishing his lunch on a bench on the edge of the school grounds, a girl walked by. Gilberto had never seen her before, but Canyon was a huge high school, and there were a lot of students he'd never seen before. She smiled shyly at him and said, "Hi."

"Hi," Gilberto answered. He felt his face flush red. He wasn't used to girls starting conversations with him, and he struggled to think of something to say. "Are you new around here?"

"Yeah, my name's Madeline," the girl said, joining him on the bench. "Most people call me 'Maddie.' "

"Hi, Maddie. I'm Gilberto." He looked at Maddie. She was skinny, too skinny. Her well-worn jeans hung loosely on her rail-thin legs. Gilberto wondered if she had an eating disorder.

"Where are you from?" he asked.

"Oh, around," Maddie answered evasively. "How about you?"

"I've lived here in Springville all my life," Gilberto answered.

"You like it?" Maddie asked. As she brushed a wisp of hair out of her eyes, Gilberto noticed that her fingernails were dirty and broken.

Gilberto shrugged. "Not really," he said.

"Me neither," Maddie said. "It's a crummy town."

Gilberto wasn't sure what to say next. He didn't know Maddie and wasn't sure whether she was looking for sympathy or just making casual conversation. Just then, the bell rang. It was time to head to his next class. "Well, I've got to go," he said, standing up. "Nice meeting you, Maddie."

"Yeah, take care," Maddie answered.

Gilberto left her sitting on the bench. Wonder where she came from, he asked himself as he headed to English class. He felt a little guilty walking away from her like that, but he had no choice. He had to get to English class.

Gilberto walked into Mr. O'Brien's class and slid into the corner desk. The other students were chatting amiably, but, as usual, Gilberto waited in silence for class to begin. To fill the time, he took out a car magazine he had in his backpack. Gilberto loved cars and bought car magazines every chance he had. He would pour over the pages, trying to decide what his dream car would be. He knew he couldn't afford the ideal car right away, but he hoped to be able to buy one after he had worked a couple of years.

As Gilberto was reading about the features of the Dodge Viper, he heard Joel French say, "Hey! My wallet's gone! I left it on my desk for just a second while I sharpened my pencil."

Gilberto looked up to see Joel staring at him. He looked around. The other desks around Joel were empty, except for the one in front of Joel, where Brandy Engberg was sitting. Besides Brandy, Gilberto was the only one close enough to have snatched the wallet. And no one would suspect Brandy. After all, she was one of the most popular girls in class. She had perfectly styled, shoulder-length auburn hair and a face like a Barbie doll. Her parents were wealthy, and she wore beautiful clothes and drove a stylish sports car. Almost all the kids were in awe of her, and most of the guys were dying to date her. There was no way anyone would accuse *her* of stealing.

Suddenly everyone was looking at Gilberto. He could feel their eyes boring into him like laser beams. They were all waiting for him to give up the wallet he'd obviously ripped off.

2

"I didn't see any wallet," Gilberto said, meeting Joel's accusing eyes.

"Hey, it didn't just walk off by itself," Joel said. "I had fifty bucks in that wallet and my driver's license. I'm not letting anybody walk away with it."

When Mr. O'Brien walked in the room, Joel told him what had happened.

"And you're certain you had your wallet when you walked in here?" Mr. O'Brien asked.

"Yes! I took it out and laid it on top of my desk for a second while I went to the pencil sharpener," Joel repeated. He turned to glare at Gilberto. "I'd sure like to see what's in his backpack. He was the only one close enough."

"I didn't take it," Gilberto protested. But, as usual, he felt like no one was listening to him.

"Gilberto, it would certainly clear the air if you'd come into my office for a few minutes," Mr. O'Brien said.

Gilberto knew that the other students were hoping Mr. O'Brien would find the wallet. It made him sick that they all assumed he was a thief even though he'd never taken anything from anyone.

He followed Mr. O'Brien into his office. Then he dumped the contents of his backpack onto Mr. O'Brien's desk. Out fell books, folders, pencils, pens, two car magazines, and three one-dollar bills. Gilberto was silent as Mr. O'Brien checked the empty backpack.

"Now how about your pockets, Gilberto?" Mr. O'Brien asked. "Can you turn them inside out for me?"

Gilberto did as he was told. Rage boiled within him, but he said nothing. Years of foster-home living had taught him to prove his innocence quickly and avoid hassles. Standing on your principles just made life harder.

"Gilberto's in the clear," Mr. O'Brien announced to the class as they returned to the classroom. He looked at Joel French. "Let's not be too hasty to accuse people from now on."

"Sorry," Joel said. Gilberto could tell Joel wasn't sincere in his apology.

As Gilberto walked by Brandy on the way to his seat, he noticed she would not look at him. She'd taken the wallet all right, he thought. Only no one would point the finger at her. No one would ask her to empty her backpack or turn her pockets inside out. Gilberto had seen it before. The "Planet Nowhere Kids" were easy scapegoats. Gilberto knew that deep down, most of the students in the room still believed he had taken the wallet and had been clever enough to hide it somewhere.

After class, Gilberto waited in the hall for Brandy. He usually avoided confrontations, but this time his anger overcame his shyness.

"I know you took Joel's wallet," he said softly when Brandy appeared. No one else heard his accusation.

"I don't know what you're talking about," Brandy said. But Gilberto could see the fear in her eyes. It was obvious she was lying.

Gilberto decided to play a hunch. "I saw you take it while Joel was sharpening his pencil," he said. "You'd better give it back."

Brandy's eyes widened, and she hurried away without saying anything more.

Gilberto waited a few seconds and then followed her down the hall. Ahead, several students from his English class were standing together talking with excitement. "Hey, Joel!" one of them called, "we found your wallet. The thief must have gotten cold feet."

Joel came running up and snatched the wallet. Quickly he checked its contents. "Looks like everything's here," he said with relief. "Did anybody see anything?"

"No, we just found the wallet lying in the middle of the hall," a student answered. Gilberto said nothing and kept walking toward them.

"Well, as long as I got my stuff back," Joel said. Just then Joel and the other students noticed Gilberto approaching. It was obvious Gilberto could not have dropped the wallet because he had not even reached the spot where they had found it. But no one said a thing. Joel didn't even bother to apologize.

Gilberto's anger seethed within him as he walked by. Joel and the other students evidently didn't think he even deserved an apology for the humiliation he had just suffered. Gilberto was part of the "Planet Nowhere" kids, and you didn't bother with kids like that.

After school, Gilberto hit the street, heading toward the Crockett house. His fists were still clenched in anger. He consoled himself with thinking about his plans for the future. Once he graduated, he'd be out of this lousy town. All he needed were a car and the open road before him. No more courts deciding what was best for him, no more foster homes, no more kids looking down on him.

When Gilberto reached the Crockett house, he went inside and hurried up the stairs to his small bedroom. Upon opening the door, he saw Mrs. Crockett going through his dresser drawers.

"What are you doing?" Gilberto demanded.

Mrs. Crockett turned around with a surprised look on her face. Gilberto had seen that same look earlier on Brandy's face. "Just putting your clean clothes in your drawer," Mrs. Crockett stammered. Gilberto could tell she was lying.

"I don't believe you," he said.

Mrs. Crockett's face became unemotional. "We have the right to search the bedrooms of our foster children any time, Gilberto. We don't want any of you kids hiding weapons or drugs in our home. It's for your protection as well as ours."

"I don't do drugs, and I don't have any weapons," Gilberto said flatly.

"I see that," Mrs. Crockett said. "So don't worry, you're not in any trouble."

Trouble? Gilberto asked himself. He had done nothing wrong. Gilberto felt violated for the second time that day. What right did she have to go through his personal belongings?

"But that's my stuff," he said. "You shouldn't be allowed to just go through it whenever you want to."

"If you've done nothing wrong, then you shouldn't mind an inspection now and then," Mrs. Crockett said. "Look at it from our perspective, Gil. A year ago we had two kids dealing drugs right out of our home. That kind of situation is dangerous for everyone living here. It's not fair to the other residents."

Gilberto sighed as he sat down on the

bed. They had him, and he knew it. He was a ward of the court, plain and simple, and had very few rights. It didn't matter that he had gotten here by being an orphan, not by breaking the law.

After Mrs. Crockett left the room, Gilberto sprang to his feet and locked the door. Then he threw himself back down on his bed and hurled his pillow at the closed door.

"You okay, Gil?" Gilberto could hear Lauren's voice just outside the door. He got up and opened it.

"Yeah, I'm fine," he said. "I just got paid a visit by Mrs. Crockett is all. She was going through my stuff."

"Looking for drugs, I'll bet," Lauren said. "She always does that. There's no privacy here, that's for sure."

"But I was never into that stuff," Gilberto protested. "It makes me mad that she suspects me without any evidence. But then that seems to be the story of my life."

"Mine too," Lauren said. "It gets old, real old. I sure wish my mom would take me back. I'm going home this weekend for a visit. Maybe I can talk her into it."

"Good luck," Gilberto said. As Lauren left the room, he got an empty, aching feeling inside. *He* had no home to go to. There was no chance he'd leave this place until he was eighteen.

* * *

The next morning, Gilberto arrived early to drama class. He wanted to tell Mr. Rhineman that there was no way he could be in the play. He decided it was a good time to ask for a place on one of the crews.

When Gilberto entered the classroom, he found Mr. Rhineman sitting at his desk listening to a cassette recording of *Othello*. The teacher turned the tape off when Gilberto approached.

"Hi, Mr. Rhineman," Gilberto began. "I just came to tell you—"

"Ah, Mr. Aguilar," Mr. Rhineman said. "I recognized your voice. How are you?"

"Um, fine," Gilberto answered. "Like I said, I just wanted to tell you that I don't think I can be in the play as that Iago guy or anyone else. Acting just isn't my thing."

"Well, that might be so, Gilberto," Mr.

Rhineman said. "But I've been reviewing your school records."

"Well, then, you know I don't do so well in school," Gilberto said. "I couldn't possibly memorize lines and stuff like that."

"On the contrary, I think you're somewhat of an underachiever," Mr. Rhineman countered. "A part in our play might be just the spark you need to get moving."

"Oh, no, that's not right," Gilberto said. "I'm not particularly good at anything, and I hate school."

"But you'd be a perfect Iago," Mr. Rhineman insisted.

"Look, I can't, Mr. Rhineman," Gilberto said. "I'm struggling in most of my classes. Being in a play would just turn up the heat."

"Are you scared, Gil?" the teacher asked gently.

"Scared? No, I'm not scared," Gilberto said. "What would I be scared of?" He tried to sound nonchalant, but his voice broke a little.

"Scared of sticking your neck out in front of the other students?" Mr. Rhineman asked. "I talked to Mr. O'Brien yesterday.

He told me what happened with the wallet. Are you afraid kids will get down on you about this?"

"I don't care what the other kids think of me," Gilberto blurted out. "I don't like them, and they don't like me. They think I'm dirt."

"Then prove to them you're not," Mr. Rhineman said. "Give this play a shot. You might just find that you've got something inside of you, some undiscovered quality that even *you* don't know about. Drama can do that for some people."

"You can't even see me, Mr. Rhineman," Gilberto said. "How do you know what I've got?"

"You know what thunder is, Gil?" the teacher asked.

"Of course," Gilberto answered.

"But have you ever *seen* it?"

"No," Gilberto admitted. "Who's ever seen thunder?"

"But you felt it, didn't you?" Mr. Rhineman asked. "And it's powerful, isn't it? That's how you strike me, Gilberto. I can feel your thunder even though I can't see it."

3

Gilberto was entirely confused by the time drama class started. Where was Mr. Rhineman coming from? How could he possibly think that Gilberto had some powerful force within him? Gilberto had always known that he was nothing special—a "Planet Nowhere" kid. If there were any special qualities within him, wouldn't they have surfaced by now?

Gilberto's thoughts were interrupted when Brandy Engberg walked by. She looked right at Gilberto and then leaned down and said, "Can I talk to you after class?"

"Yeah, sure," Gilberto replied. Now he was *really* confused.

Once he had taken attendance, Mr. Rhineman launched right into a spirited discussion of *Othello*. "Othello is the commander of the armed forces of Venice. He's a big, emotional guy who has fallen madly in love with a girl of another race, Desdemona. Desdemona is also crazy about Othello. Anyway, Othello has a very prestigious job to give out. Iago, who is an ensign serving under Othello, feels like he deserves the promotion. But Othello passes him over and gives the job to Cassio. Now the plot thickens. Iago wants revenge."

Mr. Rhineman moved back and forth across the classroom, pacing, gesturing with his white cane. "Iago makes Othello believe that Desdemona really loves Cassio. He even plants Desdemona's handkerchief on Cassio. At the thought of Desdemona's loving Cassio, Othello's blood burns 'like the mines of sulfur.' He orders Iago to kill Cassio and appoints Iago as his new lieutenant."

Surprisingly, Gilberto found himself totally caught up in the plot. It sounded like a bizarre crime story or a soap opera.

"Now, wait until you hear this," continued Mr. Rhineman. "In the meantime, Desdemona pleads with Othello to believe her innocence. But he refuses and smothers her with a pillow. By the time Othello finds out about Iago's evil plan for revenge, it's too late. Mad with grief and guilt, Othello plunges a dagger into his own heart, and Iago is taken off to jail."

"Wow, that's some story, Mr. Rhineman," Lee Wheeler said. Lee was a big shot at the school. He made it known right away that he was after the part of Othello, and Gilberto figured he'd get it.

"Okay," Mr. Rhineman said, "I want everyone in class to read a passage from the story. I'm looking for people to play parts now. We'll start with the girls."

"Do we have a choice whether we want to be actors or not?" one boy asked.

"Sorry, no," Mr. Rhineman answered. "Just look at it like it's your assignment for this unit. You *will* be graded on your performance and effort. And by the way, don't try to sabotage your readings. I already have a fairly good idea what each of you sounds like."

The rest of the class period was spent on the girls reading for parts. At the end of the hour, Mr. Rhineman said, "Okay, we got about halfway through with the readings today. We'll finish up tomorrow. See you then."

Gilberto was relieved that Mr. Rhineman hadn't gotten to him. He almost hoped that by the next day he'd be sick and wouldn't have to read. As he left the classroom, he remembered that Brandy had asked to talk to him. He lingered outside the classroom door until she came out.

"Gilberto," she said, glancing around. "Let's walk together." She lowered her voice as they headed down the hall.

"I just wanted to thank you for . . . you know, not saying anything about what happened in English class yesterday. I'm so embarrassed. I've *never* done anything like that in my whole life. And I'm sorry I got you into trouble."

Gilberto looked at her with a puzzled expression. She was a pretty girl, one of the popular kids. She was the kind of girl who dated Joel French or Lee Wheeler. She was also the kind of girl who joked about kids like Gilberto. Why was she bothering to apologize to him?

"Yeah, well," was all Gilberto could think of to say.

"You know what I think happened?" Brandy chattered on. "There's this incredible lime green blouse at Putnam's. I've been keeping my eye on it for weeks, hoping it will go on sale. Well, it did yesterday, but I didn't have the money to buy it. So I thought I'd just borrow a few dollars from Joel and then pay him back in a couple of days when I get my allowance. Joel and I are friends. I didn't think I was doing anything bad at the time, but it *was* awful, wasn't it?"

"Well . . ." Gilberto said.

"Haven't you ever wanted something really bad, Gilberto?" Brandy asked.

"Yeah, but . . ." Gilberto said. He felt funny having her call him "Gil."

"Then you know how it feels," Brandy said.

"Ever tried getting a part-time job?" Gilberto asked.

"Oh, I suppose I could," Brandy said. "But then my grades might go down, and my parents expect me to maintain a *B* average. See, Gilberto, it doesn't matter if you don't make perfect grades. No one is pressuring you."

Gilberto flinched. Even after all these years, it still hurt to be reminded that he wasn't part of a real family. Why doesn't she just tape a big sign on my back? he wondered. NOBODY WANTS THIS LOSER.

Brandy didn't seem to notice the insensitivity of her remark. "I hope you're in the play, Gilberto," she went on. "I agree with Mr. Rhineman. You'd make a wonderful Iago. There's something about your voice . . ."

But by that time, Gilberto had tuned her out. He was pretty sure she was being nice to him because he hadn't exposed her as a thief. She was probably worried that he was still considering telling Joel what had really happened.

Gilberto smiled to himself. The next thing I know, she'll be inviting me to her house. Fat chance of that ever happening, he laughed.

"I can hardly wait for drama class tomorrow so we can finish casting for the play," Brandy said when they reached her locker. "I hope I get to play Desdemona. Wouldn't it be fun if we were in the play together, Gil?"

"I guess," Gilberto said. He had to admit that being in the play with someone as pretty as Brandy might make the whole thing a little easier to take.

"See you later, Gil," Brandy said.

"Yeah, see you," Gilberto said as he walked off.

After school, Gilberto saw Mr. Rhineman leaving the building and heading toward the parking lot. Holding his cane out in front of him, the blind teacher slowly tapped his way along. Gilberto wondered how Mr. Rhineman got home. Then Mr. O'Brien appeared, and the two teachers were soon driving away in the English teacher's Blazer. No wonder Mr. Rhineman knew about the billfold incident, Gilberto thought. The two teachers probably discussed their students on the way home. Oh, well, at least it was nice that Mr. Rhineman had a friend.

Gilberto hadn't had a good friend in years. One summer when he was ten or eleven, he had lived in a foster home with Will, a tall, gentle black kid with a great sense of humor. Will could make Gilberto laugh no matter how down he was. The two friends had done everything together that summer—played baseball, rode their bikes through the park, and spent long afternoons at the community pool. But one day Will was pulled out of the foster home because an aunt had agreed to take him in. Gilberto remembered Will packing his bag in the room they had shared. "I'm going home, man!" Will had exclaimed. "To a real home. I'm going to have my own room and a dog!" Will was so excited and happy that he didn't see the sadness in his friend's face.

As Gilberto had stood waving to Will until he was out of sight, he had desperately wished he could go with him. Knowing that was impossible and also knowing that his chances of ever having a "real" home were next to nothing, Gilberto went into the house and kicked a big hole in his bedroom door. That was the worst thing he had ever done in a foster home, but now it was part of his record. He was sure Mr. and Mrs. Crockett had seen it and that it had affected their opinion of him.

Gilberto went straight to work at Hamburger Haven after school. After the dinner rush, he was standing at the counter wiping it down with disinfectant when Maddie walked in.

"You work here?" she asked.

"Yeah, I've been here for about six

months," Gilberto answered. "How are you doing?" He remembered their conversation when Maddie had told him that she hated Springville.

Maddie shrugged. "Okay, I guess. Can I have a small order of French fries?"

"Sure." Gilberto gave her the fries, and she paid for them with some dimes and nickels and a lot of pennies.

"You want something to drink?" Gilberto asked.

"Just water," Maddie answered, avoiding his eyes. She took her tray and sat down in an empty booth. Gilberto noticed that she ate the fries slowly, one at a time. As Gilberto waited on a few straggling customers, he kept glancing over at Maddie. Even though she had finished her fries, she seemed to be in no hurry to leave. She sat in the booth sipping her water and staring out the window. Suddenly Gilberto noticed that she was crying. He walked over to her booth and sat down opposite her.

"Are you okay?" he asked.

"No," Maddie replied bluntly, wiping her eyes with back of her hand. Then she picked up a napkin and blew her nose.

"You'd better go home, huh?" Gilberto asked. "It's getting late."

"There's nobody there," Maddie said in a quivering voice.

"Where is everybody?" Gilberto asked.

"There's only Mom and me, and Mom went on a trip," Maddie said, again avoiding Gilberto's eyes.

"Where do you live?" Gilberto asked.

Maddie told him.

"That's almost on my way home," Gilberto said. "I'll walk with you. I get off in a few minutes."

Maddie didn't answer him, but he noticed she remained where she was. Gilberto finished up, took off his apron, and punched out on the time clock.

"Ready?" he asked Maddie.

"Yeah," Maddie said.

"So when's your mother coming back?" Gilberto asked as they walked out into the night.

"I don't know for sure," Maddie said.

Gilberto thought that was an odd answer, but he let it go. "How old are you?" he asked, trying to keep the conversation going.

"Sixteen," Maddie said.

"I'm almost eighteen," Gilberto said.

"You're lucky," Maddie said. "You're almost old enough to be considered an adult. You'll be able to live on your own without anyone hassling you, and you won't have to go to that crummy high school." Soon they were standing in front of a large, older home with cracked paint and an overgrown front lawn. The only window Gilberto could see was boarded up. "Here's my house," Maddie said.

"Do you live here alone?" Gilberto asked.

"No," Maddie said quickly. "Why do you ask?"

"Well, from what you said earlier about my not being hassled for living alone when I'm eighteen. I was just wondering. I wouldn't tell anyone if you were."

"I told you I live with my mom," Maddie said. "I'd just *like* to live on my own, that's all. But you probably wouldn't know anything about that. You've probably got great parents waiting up for you right now."

"Actually, I live in a foster home," Gilberto admitted. "My mom's dead, and

I've never even known who my father was."

"I'm sorry, Gilberto," Maddie said. "I didn't know." She was quiet for a moment and then said, "Do you think we could be friends, Gilberto? I haven't met many people since coming here."

"Sure," Gilberto said. He liked Maddie. She was easy to talk to.

"Great," Maddie said. "Well, I've got to go, Gilberto." She started to turn toward the house but then turned back. Quickly she reached up and kissed Gilberto's cheek. "Thanks for walking me home," she said. Then she hurried up the walk.

Before Gilberto could say, "You're welcome," she was in the house with the door closed behind her.

Gilberto felt strange as he walked the few blocks to the Crockett house. His cheek was still warm where Maddie had kissed him. What was she saying by that kiss? he wondered. Did she simply need a friend? Or was she beginning to think of him as more than a friend? It gave him something nice to think about the rest of the way home.

4

The next day in drama, Mr. Rhineman had the class continue their readings. Gilberto grew more and more agitated as his turn approached. He considered deliberately blowing his lines, but then he remembered what Mr. Rhineman had said about already knowing everyone's voice pretty well.

"All right, Gilberto," Mr. Rhineman said. "Act III, Scene III, line 155."

Gilberto read,

Who steals my purse steals trash; 'tis something, nothing.

"Good," Mr. Rhineman said. "Next line."

Gilberto read on.

'Twas mine, 'til his, and has been slave to thousands;

But he that filches from me my good name

Robs me of that which not enriches him

And makes me poor indeed.

"Keep going," Mr. Rhineman said.

Gilberto read until Mr. Rhineman told him to stop. Then he glanced around. Most of the kids were watching him attentively and grinning with approval as he read. "Yeah!" Lee Wheeler cried.

Gilberto could feel his face getting red. For as long as he could remember, he had never been the center of attention like this. One part of him wanted to crawl under his desk and never come out. But, surprisingly, another part of him liked it. It made him feel special, set apart from the crowd.

"All right, class, that about does it," Mr. Rhineman said. "Give me a few minutes here, and I'll get the cast list together." He sat down at his special Braille typewriter and began to type away.

The students chatted quietly as Mr. Rhineman worked. Brandy turned to Gilberto. "You were so good," she said.

"Yeah, you're a natural," Lee said. "You make this Iago guy come alive."

Gilberto didn't know what to say. He wasn't used to other students complimenting him. "Well, I never tried anything like this before, but I kind of like it," he admitted.

"Okay, class," Mr. Rhineman said, standing up. "First of all, I'd like to thank all of you for reading. There's some real talent in this class, and I had some tough decisions to make as far as the cast goes. If you don't get a part as an actor, remember we're going to need help in other areas such as lighting and make up. There's a lot of work that goes on behind the scenes to bring a play together. Also note that from now on, class periods will be spent working on the play. And most days after school we'll also be rehearsing."

Gilberto found himself wishing that Mr. Rhineman would get on with it. He was actually hoping to hear his name read for the part of Iago.

"Brandy, you'll play the part of Desdemona," Mr. Rhineman began. "Ming, you'll be Emilia, Iago's wife. Lee, I'd like to cast you as Othello himself. Gilberto, you'll make a fine Iago."

Mr. Rhineman continued to read from his list, but Gilberto wasn't paying attention. He couldn't believe he'd landed a part in a school play. In his wildest dreams, he'd never considered such a role for himself. But what he found even more surprising was that he was actually excited about it. He realized that as he'd read the lines earlier, he had really gotten into it. There was something about this Iago character that interested him. Iago was such a classic villain. The challenge of playing him fascinated Gilberto.

Gilberto was surprised to see that both Brandy and Lee were waiting for him when the bell rang. "Mr. Rhineman is such a good teacher," Brandy said as they left the classroom.

"No kidding," Lee said. "I think it's great that he's having us put on this play. It'll be a lot of work, but I think it'll be worth it. My older sister was in a play, and she says it's the best thing she remembers from her four years at Canyon High. Say, Gilberto, maybe you could give me some help with my lines sometime. I'd like to be able to say them as naturally as you say yours."

"Sure," Gilberto said. "Be glad to." As they parted to go their separate ways, Gilberto shook his head in disbelief. A week ago he'd been just another kid from "Planet Nowhere." Now two of the most popular kids in school wanted to be his friends, *and* he had a lead in a play. He couldn't help wondering what he had done to deserve such good fortune.

At lunch, Gilberto was hoping he'd see Maddie. He wanted to tell her his good news and also see how she was doing. But the lunch period passed, and he saw no sign of her. Gilberto decided that after school he would jog over to her house and check on her.

* * *

At 3:45, Gilberto knocked on Maddie's door. A few seconds later, Maddie appeared. As Gilberto looked at her, he thought she looked more sickly than ever. Her skin was pale, her hair was dull, and she had dark circles under her eyes. "Are you okay, Maddie?" he asked. "I didn't see you at lunch today."

"Yeah, I'm fine," Maddie replied. "I just felt a little sick when I woke up, but now I'm okay."

"Is your mom home yet?" Gilberto asked, wondering why she didn't invite him in.

Maddie sighed and came outside. She sat down on the porch. "No, not yet," she said.

"Where did she go, Maddie?" Gilberto

asked, sitting next to her. He had a feeling she wasn't telling him everything.

"She went away with her boyfriend."

"When did she say she'd be back?" Gilberto asked.

"She didn't," Maddie said.

"Maddie, it's none of my business, but I don't think it's right for you to be here alone this long," Gilberto said.

Maddie's eyes widened. "You won't tell anybody, will you? Oh, please don't. My mom will be back soon. I know she will."

"I'm not going to tell anyone, Maddie," Gilberto said. "I just wish your mother would get back. Hey, who's this?"

A scrawny, yellow cat was climbing the porch steps. "This is Romeo," Maddie said, stroking the cat fondly. "And that's Juliet." She pointed at a tri-colored tabby perched on an old tree stump in the yard. "They're my best friends."

"Romeo and Juliet?" Gilbert laughed. "You like Shakespeare?"

"Yeah, we read that play when I was in ninth grade," Maddie said. She scooped up Romeo and cradled him in her arms. "It was awesome."

"I'm in a play by Shakespeare right now, *Othello*," Gilberto said. "I play the villain, Iago. We're putting it on in drama class."

"Cool," Maddie said.

"So what classes are you taking at Canyon?" Gilberto asked.

Maddie hesitated. "Oh, the usual."

"Are you a sophomore? A junior?" Gilberto asked.

"A sophomore," Maddie answered quickly. She put Romeo down and stood up. "Well, I've got to go in now. My mom might call or something."

"Okay," Gilberto said. "Hey, maybe you can come see the play."

"Maybe," Maddie said. "See you, Gil."

"'Bye, Maddie," Gilberto said, walking away. When he reached the Crocketts' house, he found Mrs. Crockett outside planting flowers.

"I'm going to be coming home a little late every night now," Gilberto told her. "On the nights I don't work at Hamburger Haven, I've got play practice."

"Play practice?" Mrs. Crockett asked, stopping her digging. "You're in a play, Gilberto?"

Gilberto could hear the surprise in her voice. For some reason, it irritated him. He felt as if she were underestimating him. But then he had to admit that he couldn't blame her. Nothing Gilberto had done so far had indicated that he had the slightest interest in anything but cars. "Yeah, we're putting on a play in drama class," he explained.

"And you're in it?" Mrs. Crockett asked again. She stood up and took off her gardening gloves. This time Gilberto realized why her question irritated him. It wasn't that she was just surprised. She was also very doubtful, as if Gilberto were lying to her. She probably thinks I'm going to be out getting into trouble, he thought.

Gilberto sighed. "The teacher's name is Mr. Rhineman, and we're doing *Othello*," he said. "You can call the school and check it out if you want."

"That's okay. I believe you, Gilberto," Mrs. Crockett said. "I'm sorry if I sounded like I didn't. Let's go tell Mr. Crockett about this. He's a real theater buff." She put her arm around Gilberto's shoulders and led him into the house.

Mr. Crockett was sitting in the living room reading the evening paper. "John," Mrs. Crockett said. "Wait 'til you hear Gil's news." She nudged Gilberto. "Go on, tell him."

Gilberto hesitated. Again he felt odd being the center of attention. "I'm in a play at school," he began.

"Great!" Mr. Crockett said. "Which play?"

"*Othello,*" Gilberto said. "I play Iago, the villain."

"*Othello?*" Mr. Crockett exclaimed. "I was in that play in college. I played Roderigo, the friend whom Iago betrays. That's a great play, Gilberto. Sit down and tell me all about it. Did you have to audition or what?"

Gilberto sat on the couch and told the Crocketts everything that had gone on in drama class that week. They listened intently as he talked, and he realized he was enjoying himself.

"You say your teacher's blind?" Mr. Crockett asked with interest. "He must be some kind of guy to teach."

"He is," Gilberto said. "He's great. All

the kids like him."

"Well, I think it's wonderful that you're in the play, Gilberto," Mrs. Crockett said. "You can bet we'll be there on opening night."

Gilberto smiled. He was surprised to find himself sharing his personal life with the Crocketts. Yesterday he was close to hating them; at best, he was indifferent to them. And he thought they felt the same way toward him. But today they didn't seem like such bad people after all. "Great," he said. "I'll look for you in the audience."

As Gilberto headed toward his room, he thought about what the Crocketts were doing with their lives. He realized that being foster parents to troubled teens would be a very tough job, and he found himself admiring them for doing it. And he supposed he couldn't blame them for taking the precautions they took. Troubled teens could be dangerous teens; he'd seen plenty of them in the various homes he'd stayed in.

Gilberto met Lauren in the hall. "Hey, Gil," she said. "I hear you got a big part in that play your drama class is putting on."

"Yeah," Gilberto said. "I play the villain."

"Great," Lauren remarked. "You'll make a good one." The two of them laughed.

Gilberto entered his room and sat down at his desk. He realized that for the first time in his life he felt like he was getting close to being a part of something. For once he was in a decent house with decent foster parents. He even had a part in a play and was on his way to making a few friends. Maybe from now on he wouldn't feel like the lost little weirdo he'd felt like for most of his life.

Gilberto wanted to write a note to Mr. Rhineman thanking him for casting him as Iago. But since Mr. Rhineman was blind, Gilberto knew a note would do no good. Then he remembered his portable cassette recorder. He took it out, inserted a blank tape, and pushed "record."

"Dear Mr. Rhineman," Gilberto began. "I didn't want to be Iago in the play *Othello*. But you pushed me into it, and now I want to thank you. You're the best teacher I've ever had. Gilberto Aguilar."

Gilberto didn't know when he'd work

up the nerve to give it to his teacher. But for now, just recording it made him feel better.

5

Gilberto started looking forward to the after-school rehearsals for *Othello*. Under Mr. Rhineman's direction, the cast worked well together, and the play began to take shape. Mr. Rhineman offered gentle criticism, helped the actors with some of the difficult language, and seemed to have as much fun as the kids.

"All right, Brandy," Mr. Rhineman said one night at practice. "Let's take it from Desdemona's line to Iago, Act II, Scene I."

Brandy began reading, looking straight at Gilberto.

"O heavy ignorance! thou praisest the worst best. But what praise couldst thou bestow on a deserving woman indeed—one that in the authority of her merit did justly put on the vouch of very malice itself?"

Gilberto took a deep breath and put on a sneer.

She that was ever fair,
and never proud,
Had tongue at will,
and yet was never loud,
Never lacked gold,

and yet went never gay,
Fled from her wish,
and yet said 'Now I may';
She that, being angered,
her revenge being nigh,
Bade her wrong stay,
and her displeasure fly.

"Excellent!" Mr. Rhineman exclaimed. "You two work great together. There's a chemistry between the two of you. Can you feel it?"

Mr. Rhineman was right. Gilberto had been feeling a sort of chemistry develop between him and Brandy. And he was pretty sure Brandy felt it too. Sometimes he caught her watching him when he wasn't looking. And then when their eyes met, instead of looking away, she would smile at him. Gilberto found himself hoping against hope that she was actually developing a fondness for him. And he knew he owed it all to Mr. Rhineman.

After one of the sessions, Gilberto slipped the cassette tape he'd recorded into Mr. Rhineman's hand.

"What's this?" Mr. Rhineman asked.

"It's sort of a note," Gilberto answered. "I mean, I had to record it because . . .

well, you know . . ."

Mr. Rhineman ignored Gilberto's uneasiness. "A note? What for?" he asked.

Gilberto hesitated. "Just for being a good teacher," he mumbled. At that moment, he was glad Mr. Rhineman couldn't see him. Gilberto was sure he had turned bright red with embarrassment just as he always did when talking to people he didn't know well.

* * *

In Gilberto's good fortune, he'd forgotten about Maddie. She hadn't come into Hamburger Haven for over two weeks, and he hadn't seen her at school. One day after play practice, he decided he'd drop by her house. He had some free time since he didn't have to work that night.

When Gilberto reached Maddie's house, he noticed that the weeds, which were bad before, had now really taken over the front yard. A middle-aged woman was whacking away at the weeds by the porch. Gilberto assumed it was Maddie's mother and was relieved to see that she had finally made it home. But he hesitated before approaching her. Just then the woman happened to glance up. "Can I help you?" she asked.

"Um, I was just wondering if Maddie's home," Gilberto said.

"Maddie? Who's Maddie?" the woman asked.

"I thought maybe you were her mom," Gilberto said.

"No, I'm a real estate agent," the woman replied. "This house is vacant, and I'm trying to sell it. You don't do yard work, do you?" She whacked at another bunch of weeds. This time she exposed a "For Sale" sign that Gilberto hadn't noticed before.

Vacant? Gilberto wondered. Maddie had said she lived here with her mother. Then her fear-stricken face came to Gilberto's mind. "You won't tell anybody, will you? Oh, please don't."

It dawned on Gilberto that Maddie was probably a runaway, a homeless kid camping out in a vacant house. He didn't want to say too much for fear of exposing her. "Uh, no," Gilberto said. "I already have a job. But thanks for asking."

As he headed toward home, Gilberto wondered where Maddie was now. Did she have anxious parents who were searching for her? Or was she like Gilberto, with no parents at all? Either way, would she return to the house once the real estate agent had gone? Gilberto made up his mind to walk by the house periodically in case Maddie came back.

When he got home, he told Mrs. Crockett about Maddie without actually mentioning her name. "What can I do to help her without getting her busted and tossed in juvenile detention?" he asked.

"I know some good people in the Department of Social Services, Gil," Mrs. Crockett said. "There's a real nice lady in the child protective office named Marge Tolliver. Here, let me get her card." She left the room for a minute and came back carrying a business card.

"The next time you see your friend, you tell her to call Marge," Mrs. Crockett said. "She'll come have a chat with her. No police. No pressure. No getting busted. She's a great lady."

"Thanks," Gilberto said, putting the

card in his wallet. Gilberto had dealt with the Department of Human Services many times as well, but always as a ward of the state. It felt good to have the name of someone with some "pull" who might be able to help Maddie.

* * *

Gilberto was still wondering about Maddie the next day at lunch. He decided he'd drop by the vacant house again that evening after work. As he sat eating his sandwich, Brandy joined him.

"Hi," Brandy said, sitting down and opening her carton of milk. "The play's going great, huh?"

"Um, yeah," Gilberto said.

"I still can't get over what an evil character Iago is," Brandy said. "I don't know when I've seen a more evil villain."

Brandy's comment led them to a discussion of movies they'd seen with particularly nasty villains. As they talked and laughed, Gilberto decided that this was his chance to ask Brandy out.

"Um, Brandy," Gilberto said, "speaking

of movies, do you think the two of us might go see one sometime?"

Brandy didn't hesitate. "That'd be great," she said.

Gilberto thought for a moment that he was dreaming. Had she *really* said yes, or had he imagined it? He decided to find out. "Would Friday be okay? I don't work that night."

"Perfect," Brandy said. "I just love movies."

"Great," Gilberto managed to say as they finished their lunches and headed out of the cafeteria.

"See you later, Gil," Brandy said.

Stunned, Gilberto walked to his next class. This beautiful, popular girl whose father was a big shot in town had actually agreed to go out with him. Brandy wasn't Maddie, a lonely little waif who had practically begged for his friendship. And Brandy wasn't Lauren with the sad, sullen eyes who shared Gilberto's foster home history. This was Brandy Engberg, who high stepped through a boy's fantasies like a drum majorette, always out of reach.

Gilberto tried to remember when he

had been this happy. To find that time, he had to reach back to the last day he had spent with his mother. They had gone to an amusement park and ridden a giant roller coaster called "The Tidal Wave." Gilberto and his mother had screamed all the way down the giant dips and clung to each other laughing when the coaster climbed the seemingly endless peaks. Gilberto had been 7, and his mother was 23, a dark-haired, laughing girl who had managed to put all her demons behind her that day. It was as if the two of them had stepped into the pages of a fairy tale. They ate corn dogs and strawberry malts, laughed at the hall of mirrors, and got soaking wet on the water rides. It was the happiest day of Gilberto's childhood. Four days later, his mother had died.

But Gilberto decided that today he wouldn't be sad about what had happened. Today he would only remember the fun he'd had with his mother. After all, he had a lot to be thankful for. Hadn't a beautiful girl just agreed to go out with him? Dwelling on the past would only take him backward, not forward.

* * *

Gilberto had to work late that night because two other employees had called in sick. By the time he left Hamburger Haven, it was almost eleven o'clock. It was raining, and as he headed toward Maddie's house, he hoped that if she wasn't there, she was at least out of the rain.

When he reached the house, he saw that the windows were dark. The house showed every sign of being vacated. He stood staring at it for a few minutes, wondering if he should knock at the door. But then he decided that if the neighbors saw him, he would arouse too much suspicion.

He shook his head sadly. Where was she? he wondered. Was she safe? Was she dry? Was she alone somewhere?

Just as he turned to go, he saw a light flicker inside the house. For a minute he thought it was his imagination, but then he saw a yellow cat jump up into the windowsill and stretch out. Romeo, he thought.

Gilberto smiled. Maddie had found her

way into the house again. She was out of the rain for now. That was enough for him tonight, and he went home.

6

Gilberto promised Mr. Crockett that he would mow the lawn for a month if he could borrow Mr. Crockett's car for his date with Brandy. Mr. Crockett was reluctant. He treasured his old Volvo, but he hated mowing lawns, so he agreed. "Be careful, Gil," he said. "That old car's like a friend to me."

"You can trust me," Gilberto assured him, grabbing the car keys. He was grateful for the year he'd spent in the Fowler foster home before he came to live with the Crocketts. He had been expected to take an aged grandmother to her monthly doctor's appointment, so he left that home with a driver's license.

Gilberto drove to the pretty Spanish-style house on the hill where the Engbergs lived. When he knocked on the front door, Mr. Engberg let him in. Gilberto noticed that the older man was polite but cold to him, as if he wasn't too happy to see Brandy leave with such a boy. "Brandy, I expect you home by 10:00," were his last words to Brandy as the two left the house.

In the car on the way to the theater, Gilberto said, "Your father didn't seem too thrilled about my taking you out."

Brandy rolled her eyes and said, "Dad is such a snob. He'd rather I stick to our little social circle. He wants me to date boys whose families live in the hills around here and whose fathers play golf with him. The higher up on the hill people live, the more stuck-up they are. They're all so boring. I'd much rather be with you because you're different."

"Should I take that as a compliment?" Gilberto asked, smiling.

"Of course," Brandy answered. "Dad's always saying, 'The apple doesn't fall too far from the tree.' It's his way of saying that good kids come from good families, and bad kids come from families with problems. I used to agree with him until I met you. I don't care what happened that caused you to end up in foster care. I really like you."

Gilberto wondered if Brandy was fishing for information or just making conversation. He decided she probably did want to know something about him. "My parents," he began, "well, I never knew my father, but my mom died when I was seven."

"Oh," Brandy said. "That's so sad. She must have been very young."

"She was 23," Gilberto said. He remembered his young mother's face and voice, her soft, curly hair, and her giggle that was so contagious. He had a photo of her in his wallet. It was her graduation picture, but she hadn't changed much from the time she was a senior and the time she died. Now he fished in his wallet and handed the photo to Brandy.

"She was so pretty," Brandy exclaimed. "How did she die?"

Gilberto's mouth turned dry. His mother had died of a drug overdose, an accidental mixture of drugs and liquor. But Gilberto didn't want to tell Brandy that. He felt it would be like insulting his mother. So he said, "Cancer. She died of cancer."

"I'm so sorry," Brandy said. "That must have been awful for you, Gil."

"Yeah," Gilberto said. "It was. But I'm doing all right now." He turned down the street toward the theater. "I'm really looking forward to seeing this movie," he added, wanting to change the subject. He wanted his first date with Brandy to be fun, not depressing.

"Me too," Brandy said. "I just love the two stars."

Soon they were settled in their seats with a tub of popcorn and two colas. The movie was a romance, and it made Gilberto want to put his arm around Brandy, but he decided not to. He didn't want her to think he was coming on too strong. But halfway through the movie, Brandy slipped her hand into his. He glanced over at her. Through the dim light cast by the screen, Gilberto could see her smiling at him. He let go of her hand and put his arm around her, pulling her closer to him. She laid her head on his shoulder and stayed that way for the rest of the show.

The movie got over at 9:40, so Gilberto had just enough time to get Brandy home before 10:00. As he walked her to the door, she said, "I had a great time tonight, Gil."

"So did I," Gilberto said. He wanted to kiss her goodnight, but he thought it was too soon. So at the front door, he said, "Well, so long, Brandy."

"Good-bye, Gil," Brandy said. But before she turned to go, she reached up and kissed him lightly on the lips. "See you at school, Iago," she smiled.

"Okay, Desdemona," Gilberto laughed. On the drive home, Gilberto was amazed at the warmth and friendliness Brandy had shown him that night. She really *did* like him. The future looked so bright. They'd go on other dates and get to know each other better and better. And there would be all those play rehearsals. Gilberto couldn't believe his good fortune.

* * *

On Saturday morning, Gilberto walked over to Maddie's house. He wanted to give her the name of the person from Department of Human Services. But as he approached the house, he was shocked to see a police car in the driveway. Gilberto saw the realtor he had talked to earlier standing on the front porch. She looked very agitated.

"What's going on?" Gilberto asked.

"Some transient has been hanging out

in this house, making herself at home," the real estate agent said, shaking her head.

Just then a policewoman came through the front door leading Maddie by the arm. Maddie was crying, and her hair was tangled as if she had just awakened. Her big eyes were wild with fear.

"Gilberto!" she cried as she was led past.

"It's okay, Maddie," Gilberto said. "I'll get you some help. I've got the name of a lady from Social Services."

"My cats!" Maddie cried. "Take care of my cats!"

"I will," Gilberto shouted before she disappeared into the squad car.

Gilberto rushed to the nearest pay phone and dialed the number on the business card. It was Saturday, but he thought there might be a chance that she was in her office.

"Marge Tolliver," a woman's voice said.

"My name is Gilberto Aguilar," Gilberto said. "My foster mother, Mrs. Crockett, gave me your name. She said you help kids in trouble."

"Oh, yes, I know Mrs. Crockett," Marge said. "What can I do for you, Gilberto?"

"I've got a friend, Maddie," Gilberto said. "I think she's a runaway. She was just picked up by the police. I guess they're taking her to juvenile hall. Could you, like, go there now and help her? She's really desperate, Ms. Tolliver. She doesn't have anyone else."

"I think that can be arranged," Marge said. "Give me your name again and your home phone number for my records."

Gilberto complied. "So you'll go there today?" he asked.

"As soon as I finish up this paperwork," Marge said. "I should be able to make it there before noon."

"Great!" Gilberto said. "Thanks a lot. Oh, and Ms. Tolliver, do you think there's a chance Maddie could be placed in a foster home? Because if so, it would be great if she could come to the Crocketts' house. They're really nice people."

"I'll see what I can do," Marge said. "I'll call you later and let you know what happens, Gilberto."

Gilberto returned to the vacant house

and picked up the two cats. He headed home carrying a cat in each arm. When he got to the Crocketts' house, he found the couple on the front porch drinking coffee.

"What do you have there, Gil?" Mrs. Crockett said.

Gilberto told them what happened. "So do you think we could keep the cats until we find out what happens with Maddie?" he asked.

"I don't know," Mr. Crockett said hesitantly. "I've never been very fond of cats."

"Nonsense," Mrs. Crockett said. "You've never had one, that's all. You have to have one to appreciate them." She turned to Gilberto. "You can keep them, Gilberto. But they have to stay in the garage, and you'll have to buy their food from the money you make at Hamburger Haven. Deal?"

Gilberto smiled. That was fair enough, he decided. "Deal," he said. Then he asked, "So do you think Maddie will be placed in foster care?"

"That depends on the County," Mr. Crockett said. "But there's a pretty good chance, at least temporarily."

Gilberto got the cats settled into the

garage, but he worried about Maddie all day. She had seemed so afraid when he had seen her this morning. Maybe she'd actually broken some law by staying in that house. Maybe they'd throw her in a reformatory instead of placing her in foster care.

On Sunday afternoon, Marge Tolliver called Gilberto. "I talked to Maddie," Marge said. "She's doing okay, so you can stop worrying about her. Tomorrow morning she'll start going through the process with Human Services, and they'll decide what to do with her. I told them about the Crocketts, so let's keep our fingers crossed."

"Thanks, Ms. Tolliver," Gilberto said. "Did she ask about her cats?"

"She told me her friend Gilberto had promised to take care of them," Marge said with a smile in her voice.

* * *

On Monday morning, Gilberto told Brandy about Maddie.

"The poor thing," Brandy said. "It's so

nice of you to try to help her. That's what I keep telling my dad. That you don't have to be rich to be a good person."

Gilberto noticed that Brandy was wearing a new cashmere sweater. It was soft pink, and she looked great in it. "Hey, that sweater looks nice on you," he told her.

Brandy smiled. "Thanks. I just love cashmere, but it's so expensive. Mom and Dad are on this responsibility kick. They're making me buy my own clothes for a while 'so I appreciate the value of a dollar,' they said." She stroked one of the sleeves. "Now I need some pants to match. I saw a pair in Putnam's, but they were a hundred dollars. I'm going to keep my eye on them to see if they go on sale. They'll go perfect with this sweater."

Gilberto could see in Brandy's eyes how much she adored her sweater and how much she wanted the slacks to match. It worried him that she could look so desperate about clothing. He remembered something he'd pushed far back into his mind—the time Brandy took Joel French's wallet so she could buy a blouse she wanted. But the memory was so unpleasant that he quickly made up his mind not to think about it.

7

Every afternoon, Gilberto and the rest of the drama students rehearsed *Othello*, worked on the sets and lighting, and generally had a wonderful time. Mr. Rhineman sometimes had pizza brought in, and other times the various students brought snacks. Little by little, they were fusing into a sort of family, more of a family than Gilberto had known since his mother died.

A tough kid named Mason turned out to be a whiz at painting the background for the scenes and designing the sets. He and his crew created Venice, Italy, and the island of Cyprus using plywood, odds and ends, and splashes of creatively applied paint. A shy, quiet girl named Amy worked magic with the lighting, and Ming, Brandy's friend, was an excellent costume designer. And there was always Mr. Rhineman suggesting a change in tone of voice to convey more emotion here, underplaying a scene there. Mr. Rhineman couldn't see Mason's wonderful sets, but he seemed to visualize them and even offered tips on how to improve them. He couldn't see how Amy worked the lights or the costumes Ming designed, but he knew instinctively what worked and what didn't. After a while, Gilberto and the rest of the students forgot that their teacher was blind. And when, occasionally, Mr. Rhineman bumped into something that had been moved from its usual spot, no one laughed. They simply offered apologies and corrected the problem so it didn't happen again.

The dress rehearsal was scheduled for Wednesday night, and the play would actually be staged Thursday and Friday evenings. Gilberto got special permission from his boss at hamburger Haven to have the three nights off.

An article in the local newspaper listed all the cast members. Gilberto proudly showed it to Mr. and Mrs. Crockett.

"So you're really in it, Gil," Mrs. Crockett said, nodding her head. "I'm sorry again if I doubted you about this. We're really proud of you."

The article went on to tell about Mr. Rhineman's earlier career as an actor on Broadway. It stated that Mr. Rhineman had a congenital eye disease and that by the age of thirty, he was blind. It was at that point that he turned to teaching as an outlet for his creativity. Gilberto was glad that he had.

On Wednesday morning, Gilberto could hardly contain his excitement as he headed to school. He didn't even think about Maddie very much. Tonight was the night Gilberto Aguilar would play Iago, the most fascinating villain in literature.

The day went by slowly for Gilberto. The only thing that made it tolerable at all was seeing Brandy.

"I'm so nervous about tonight," Brandy said to Gilberto as they walked into drama class. "What if I forget my lines?"

"Tell me about it," Gilberto agreed.

Mr. Rhineman must have heard their discussion because when the bell rang, he said, "Don't worry about tonight, kids. This dress rehearsal is a chance for you to get the feel of working before a real audience. It's to prepare you for the actual performances on Thursday and Friday. If you forget your lines, Abdul is in the wings waiting to cue you."

The cast members all glanced at

Abdul gratefully.

"I think we've got a really good show here," Mr. Rhineman went on. "Over the last few weeks you students have shown me talent that I didn't even know existed in this classroom. I'm confident that we're going to pull this thing off without a hitch."

Gilberto sighed. He sure hoped Mr. Rhineman was right. He was starting to believe that maybe he wasn't just one of the kids from Planet Nowhere. This was his chance to prove it to himself and everybody else.

At 5:45 that afternoon, Gilberto prepared to go to the school. He was supposed to report to the auditorium an hour before the play started.

"You're sure you're coming?" he'd asked Mr. and Mrs. Crockett as he left the house.

"Wouldn't miss it for the world," Mrs. Crockett said. "Now go on. You're going to be late."

"Hey, Gil," Mr. Crockett called as Gilberto started down the sidewalk. "Break a leg!"

"Thanks," Gilberto said with a wave.

When Gilberto arrived at the auditorium, it was a flurry of activity. Mason and his crew were putting the finishing touches on the last background set. Amy and her crew were testing the headsets they would use to communicate during the performance. And Ming was stitching the hem of Brandy's dress as Brandy rehearsed her lines with Lee.

Gilberto quickly changed into his costume and went to the make up room where the crew was waiting to make him look as villainous as possible. When they were done, he went back to the boys' dressing room and stood in front of the full-length mirror. He liked what he saw. The crew had given him bushy black eyebrows and a mustache and goatee. On his head was a cap with a red feathered plume, and he wore a black cape trimmed in red across his shoulders. But best of all, he carried a long, shiny sword with a jeweled hilt. It was only a prop, but it looked real enough. In Act V, he would use this sword to "stab" Roderigo, the friend whom Iago betrays, and Cassio, the man who got the job Iago wanted.

At 6:55, Gilberto peeked out from behind the curtain. The auditorium was packed, but he spotted Mr. and Mrs. Crockett sitting in the second row. It made him feel good to know that they must have come really early to get seats that close.

At seven o'clock, Mr. Rhineman stepped onto the stage and stood in front of the closed curtain. He looked splendid in his aristocratic costume from 16th century Venice. "Ladies and gentlemen," he announced. "I am delighted to present to you the first performance this year by the drama students at Canyon High. Tonight you will see a fresh, vital, and marvelous group of young people, most without any previous dramatic experience. Over the weeks, these students have come together in a magical ensemble. It is with unabashed pride that I give you *Othello*, written by William Shakespeare and performed by the drama students of Canyon High School."

As the audience applauded, the curtain rose, and for a minute Gilberto felt like he was in someone else's dream. Surely it wasn't he who was going out on that stage in front of all those people! But as he strode onto center stage, it was as if some powerful force controlled him. He heard his own voice raging against the injustice Othello had visited upon him: "By the faith of man, I know my price, I am worth no worse a place."

For the rest of the play, Gilberto was totally immersed in his character and in the plot of the story. It was as if he really was Iago, Lee was Othello, and Brandy was Desdemona. A couple of times Gilberto and some of the other characters hesitated on their lines, but, as Mr. Rhineman had promised, Abdul was always there to provide the needed cues. By the end of the play, Gilberto and everyone involved knew they had "pulled it off," maybe not totally without a hitch, but pulled it off, nevertheless.

One by one the cast members took their bows, starting with the minor characters. The audience clapped in appreciation. But when Lee, Brandy, and Gilberto joined hands and stood center stage, the audience rose to its feet and cheered loudly. Gilberto could hardly believe his eyes. A standing ovation! And in the second row stood Mr. and Mrs. Crockett cheering as loudly as anyone. Gilberto's heart swelled as he saw Mrs. Crockett dab at her eyes with a handkerchief.

The next two nights went even better than the dress rehearsal. On Friday night after the final performance, the cast and crew had a huge party in the gymnasium at the school. Piles of catered food were brought in, and the atmosphere was festive. Gilberto found himself laughing with Brandy, Lee, and the other students as if he'd known them all his life. Everyone was already asking Mr. Rhineman what the next play would be.

"Hold on!" he said, laughing. "I thought you didn't like doing plays."

"That was before," Brandy said.

"Yeah, before you came," Lee agreed.

"We just might have time for one more before the end of the year," Mr. Rhineman said. "How about a comedy this time?"

"It depends," Gilberto said, twisting his mustache. "Are there any villains in it?" Everyone laughed.

Gilberto had managed to get the Volvo again, so he drove Brandy home after the party.

"What a great time we had," Brandy sighed as she leaned her head on Gilberto's shoulder. "I just loved being Desdemona."

"And you were great," Gilberto said.

"I can't believe it's really over," Brandy went on. "It makes me sad. I'll bet we remember this for the rest of our lives, Gil. When we're old and gray, we'll be sitting in our rocking chairs saying, 'Do you remember that first play we were in together?' "

Gilberto smiled. It felt good to hear Brandy imagining the two of them together so many years later.

Gilberto made up his mind that this time when he walked Brandy to the door, he would kiss her goodnight. But when they reached the porch, the front door opened, and Mrs. Engberg appeared in the doorway.

"Is that you, Brandy?" she asked.

"Yes, Mom," Brandy said. "Gilberto brought me home."

Gilberto saw a look of distinct distaste appear on the older woman's face. "Um, hi, Mrs. Engberg," he said. "Did you get to see the play?"

"Yes, we saw it last night," Mrs. Engberg said, in a chilly voice.

"Wasn't Gil fabulous, Mom?" Brandy said. "Everybody was raving about how good he was."

"Yes," Mrs. Engberg said, taking Brandy's arm and pulling her into the house. "Now goodnight, Gilberto."

The door closed quickly. Gilberto was about to leave when he heard Mrs. Engberg's voice, louder than before. "He's not your boyfriend, is he, Brandy?" she asked.

"Oh, Mom! He's perfectly nice," Brandy said.

"Well, when courts put children in foster homes, it's not because they're choir boys," Mrs. Engberg declared.

"Mom, he's an orphan. His mother died," Brandy protested. "Are you going to hold that against him?"

"That's the story he told you, but how do you know it's true?" Mrs. Engberg countered. "He looks like one of those gang members you see on television."

"You can be such a bigot!" Brandy cried. "You don't like him because his last name is Aguilar instead of Worthington!"

"That's not true, Brandy," Mrs. Engberg said. "The Galvez family has been close to use for years. If you were dating Peter Galvez, I'd be pleased."

"Yeah, because Mr. Galvez is a millionaire," Brandy said. "Just because Gilberto isn't rich doesn't mean he's not a good person, one that I'd be proud to call my boyfriend."

"You're just trying to be rebellious, young lady, and I don't appreciate it," Mrs. Engberg said. "You think it's exciting to date a 'bad boy' but—"

Brandy cut her off before she could finish. "Gilberto's not a bad boy!" she said. "That is just so stupid to think that."

Gilberto didn't hear anything more because he turned and headed toward the car. He was momentarily sad at what he'd heard. But then he thought, So what if Mrs. Engberg doesn't like me? Brandy likes me, and that's all that counts for now!

8

When Gilberto got home after the party, Mrs. Crockett was waiting up for him. "I've got good news for you, Gil," she said.

"What?" Gilberto asked with dread. The last time he had heard those words from a foster parent, he'd been told he was on his way to another home, one that would "better meet his needs."

"Don't look so worried," Mrs. Crockett laughed. "It's Maddie. She's coming to stay here for a while. Ms. Tolliver is bringing her over in the morning."

Maddie? Gilberto wondered. In the excitement of the week, he'd nearly forgotten about her. "Really? Maddie's coming here?" he cried. "That's great. You'll really like her, Mrs. Crockett. She's a nice girl."

The next morning at 9:30, a car pulled into the Crocketts' driveway. A tall, stately black woman stepped out of the driver's seat, and Maddie got out on the passenger side. Gilberto was watching from the window. Now he ran out the front door.

"Maddie!" he called as he descended the porch steps. A smile flickered on

Maddie's face when she saw Gilberto. "Are my cats okay?" she asked.

"Yeah, they're doing fine," Gilberto said. "They'll be glad to see you. I am too." He turned to Marge Tolliver. "I'm Gilberto," he said. "The one who called you."

"And I'm Marge Tolliver," the woman said. "This is the boy you have to thank for getting you here," she said to Maddie.

"Thanks, Gil," Maddie said. Gilberto picked up one of Maddie's bags and headed toward the house. He introduced Maddie to the Crocketts and then took her upstairs to her bedroom. Ms. Tolliver and the Crocketts stayed downstairs to take care of the necessary paperwork involved in taking in a foster child.

"You'll be in here with Lauren," Gilberto said as he opened the bedroom door. "She's real nice. She's visiting her mother again this weekend."

Maddie sat down on the bed. "This is nice," she said shyly. She seemed ill at ease in her new surroundings.

Gilberto sat down next to her. "So how are you?" he asked. "Are you okay?"

"I'm fine," Maddie said. "Just a little

stressed out from the week. It was scary when the police came and got me out of that house."

"I'll bet," Gilberto said. He tried to think of something that would make her feel more comfortable. "Hey, do you want to see your cats?" he asked.

"Sure," Maddie said. She followed him outside to the garage. "Romeo!" she cried, picking up the yellow tomcat.

"And here's Juliet," Gilberto said scooping up the small tabby. "Let's go sit on the porch with them."

Once they reached the porch, Maddie asked, "How did your play turn out?"

"Great," Gilberto answered. "It was a lot of fun."

"I'm glad," Maddie said. "I saw your name in the paper."

"Yeah, I'm a big star now, huh?" Gilberto laughed. "You sure like these cats, don't you?"

"They're all I've got," Maddie said, cuddling Romeo.

It dawned on Gilberto that he really knew nothing about this girl. Was she a runaway? Or was she an orphan like himself? Or both? He decided he'd try to find out. "Um, Maddie," he said. "You know, my mother is dead. Is it true what you told me about your mom—that she went off with her boyfriend and left you alone?"

"No," Maddie said.

"Do you have parents, Maddie?" Gilberto asked softly.

Maddie nodded slowly. "Yeah," she said. "They live in Connecticut in a big, two-story house with an apple orchard and a collie dog named Shep."

Gilberto wasn't sure if she was being sarcastic or telling the truth. "You do?" he asked. "Really?"

"Yes, really," Maddie said.

"Why aren't you living with them, Maddie?" Gilberto asked. He couldn't imagine anyone not wanting to live in such an ideal place.

Maddie shrugged her shoulders. Then she said, "I got in with a bad crowd a couple of years ago. Mom and Dad weren't happy about it. I started climbing out my bedroom window at night while they were asleep. Once they found out, they tried to punish me, but all it did was make me resent them. Finally I couldn't stand it anymore, and I just took off."

"All by yourself?" Gilberto asked.

"Yeah," Maddie said. "They caught me a couple of times and took me back home. So I just ran farther and faster each time until they couldn't find me. I've been on my own for almost a year now."

"Man," Gilberto said. "It's been rough, huh?"

Maddie nodded, blinking back tears.

"Did Ms. Tolliver call your parents and tell them you were here?" Gilberto asked.

"Yeah, but they don't want me back," Maddie said, her words turning bitter. "My parents are older. They didn't have me until they were almost fifty. Anyway, Dad had a stroke after I left. Now he's sort of like an invalid. Mom blames me. And she told Ms. Tolliver that with Dad's health problems, she didn't see how they could handle me anymore."

Gilberto didn't know what to say. He felt sorry for Maddie, but he felt sorry for her parents too. He had always heard that parents are supposed to love their children no matter what. But he figured that was just a fairy tale. No one can go on loving someone who doesn't love them back.

"Anyway," Maddie said, forcing a weak smile. "I'm going to be all right. Ms. Tolliver said that if things work out, I might be able to stay with the Crocketts until I graduate. I'm enrolling at Canyon High next week after they get all the paperwork done on me. I'm going to try real hard to get good grades."

"That's great," Gilberto said.

"Yeah, maybe I can stop being such a loser now and do something real cool like you did being in that play," Maddie said.

"You bet," Gilberto said. "Maybe you can get into Mr. Rhineman's class."

"I'm no good at acting," Maddie said.

"I didn't think I was either until Mr. Rhineman convinced me to give it a try," Gilberto said. He smiled then and passed on Mr. Rhineman's mother's advice. "After all, Maddie, you never know what you can do until you try."

* * *

Since play practice was over, Brandy asked Gilberto if he wanted to go to the mall with her Monday after school.

"Sure," Gilberto said. "I don't have to work tonight, and I don't think Mr. Crockett needs the car. I'll pick you up in an hour."

"Great," Brandy said. "Putnam's is having a one-day sale. A lot of their stuff is fifty percent off. I'm hoping those pink pants that I want are on sale. My grandmother gave me some money, and I've got just enough to buy them if they're fifty percent off."

Gilberto managed to get Mr. Crockett's Volvo and drove over to pick up Brandy. When they reached the mall, Gilberto wasn't much interested in following Brandy around the juniors department of Putnam's Department Store. Instead he stayed downstairs where they had video games. He finished an entire level of "Dragon's Doom" when he realized that Brandy was taking an awfully long time to buy those slacks. He rode up the escalator to the juniors department and walked over to the sales counter where an older lady was hanging up a pair of pink slacks.

"I'm waiting for someone who's trying on clothes," he said. "Her name's Brandy Engberg. Is she still here?"

The woman had a strange look on her face. "There's a little problem," she said tersely.

"Problem? Is she okay?" Gilberto asked. He was beginning to feel a little uncomfortable. What was going on?

"You'd better check at the office," the woman said. She pointed to the big Customer Service sign on the opposite side of the store. "Over there."

Gilberto rushed over to the office, almost colliding with a mannequin in his haste. A girl sat at a computer working on invoices. She looked up. "Can I help you?"

"Yes, I think my friend is here," Gilberto said. "Brandy Engberg."

Before the girl could answer, a door opened and Brandy emerged. Her face was streaked with mascara, and she was wiping her eyes with a tissue.

"Brandy!" Gilberto cried. "What happened?"

"Oh, Gilberto," Brandy sobbed, grabbing

his arm. "Let's get out of here. They're saying I tried to steal a pair of slacks."

"What?" Gilberto gasped.

"I tried on those slacks I told you about, and then I started walking into another area of the store," Brandy explained as they made their way down the aisle to the elevator. "The lady in the juniors department nabbed me and marched me off to the office."

"But why didn't you pay for the slacks right away?" Gilberto asked.

"I wanted to look at some other things, maybe try a few more things on," Brandy said. "I was going to pay for them. Honest! Oh, Gilberto, I could just die. They called my parents and everything. My whole life is ruined."

"Take it easy, Brandy," Gilberto said. Just then they passed the juniors department. Next to the aisle was a rack of pink slacks. At the top of the rack was a sale sign that read "33% Off."

Gilberto felt his heart sinking. "Are those the ones you wanted?" he asked.

"Yes," Brandy said, obviously not noticing the sign. "And now I'll never have them."

At 33 percent off, Gilberto knew that Brandy hadn't had enough money to purchase the slacks. She had only brought $50 with her, and the slacks would have cost around $67. Again Gilberto remembered the incident with Joel French's wallet.

As they headed down the escalator, Gilberto asked, "Brandy, did you tell them you'd pay for the slacks?"

"Yeah. I mean no, Brandy stammered, not looking at him. Then she added quickly, "It wouldn't have done any good. They were all mad at me by that time."

By the time they reached the parking lot, Gilberto thought he had pretty much figured out what had happened. When Brandy had seen that the slacks were only 33 percent off, she was so overcome with disappointment that she had tried to steal them. She probably planned to tell her mother that she had paid fifty dollars for them. But she never got the chance.

Gilberto felt sick on the drive home. He had felt so flattered when Brandy had started paying attention to him. He had hoped against hope that maybe something would develop between them. The chemistry between them was so strong. Even Mr. Rhineman had said so. But everything that had gone so right for the last few weeks now seemed terribly wrong. This beautiful and perfect girl—this girl of his dreams, the one he would do anything for—was a thief.

9

Gilberto pulled into the driveway of the beautiful house on the hill. Just before she got out of the car, Brandy said, "Do you think you could come in with me? It might make it a little easier to face my parents."

"Sure," Gilberto said, "if you think it will help." Even though it was obvious Brandy had a problem, he felt sorry for her and wanted to help her if possible.

Gilberto was amazed at the evidence of wealth he saw as they entered the house. The entryway was at least thirty feet high, and from the ceiling hung a huge crystal chandelier. A fountain splashed merrily in the middle of the entryway, and a winding and ornate staircase led to the floor above. And this is only the entryway! he marveled. Why would anyone who lived with such luxuries need to steal?

"Come on," Brandy said. "They're probably in the family room."

Gilberto followed her obediently, still amazed by the furnishings he saw as he passed through the house. When they reached the family room, Mr. and Mrs. Engberg were sitting on a plush, wrap-around sofa. Both immediately stood and glared at Brandy as she entered the room.

"You'd better have a good explanation for what happened tonight, Brandy," Mr. Engberg said, anger apparent in his voice.

Brandy seemed to crumple under their glares, and her tears returned. "Mom! Dad!" she cried. "I didn't do anything. It was all a mistake, a terrible mistake. I was going to pay for the slacks. They just didn't give me a chance."

Suddenly Mr. Engberg spotted Gilberto. His eyes narrowed with distrust. "Go to your room, Brandy," he demanded.

"But Dad—" Brandy protested.

"Do as your father asks," Mrs. Engberg said coldly. "We'll be up to deal with you later."

"'Bye, Gil," Brandy said sadly as she turned to go.

"You are not to have any more to do with our daughter," Mr. Engberg said to Gilberto when Brandy had gone. "Do you understand?"

"I hear what you're saying," Gilberto answered, "but I don't understand."

"Don't play games with us," Mrs. Engberg said. "Brandy has always been a model child—honest, trustworthy. She hasn't given us a bit of trouble. Then she took up with you, and suddenly she's been accused of stealing from a department store—*while you were with her.*"

"But I didn't do anything," Gilberto began. "In fact, you might want to seek—"

"Enough!" Mr. Engberg cut in. "We are under no illusions about your background, young man. You are likely to be very familiar with the criminal justice system. And now you've drawn an innocent girl into your pattern of illegal behavior."

"Wait a minute," Gilberto said. "I've never stolen anything in my life. I've got nothing to do with what happened tonight. I was downstairs playing video games when Brandy got busted."

"Busted?" Mr. Engberg cried. "Are you insinuating that Brandy took those slacks?"

"Well, actually . . ." Gilberto began.

"Don't be ridiculous, John," Mrs. Engberg said. "He's just trying to get himself off the hook." She glared at

Gilberto. "The minute I saw you, I knew you were trouble, young man. I tolerated your hanging around Brandy during the play. But now that the play is over, so is your friendship with our daughter. You are not to go near Brandy again. Is that understood?"

Gilberto nodded his head sadly.

"And if you do," Mr. Engberg said, "we can make it very uncomfortable for you. We're very aware of your current situation. I'm sure you'd much rather stay in that foster home you're in than go to a reform school. Am I right?"

Again Gilberto nodded. They had him, and they knew it. If the Engbergs claimed that he had made trouble for Brandy, the Crocketts could request that he leave. And with only a few months left until he turned eighteen, the state might just put him in reform school rather than find another foster home for him.

Mr. Engberg accompanied him to the front door. "Don't forget what we said, young man," he said. "Stay away from Brandy—for good."

Gilberto was stunned as he drove the

Volvo back to the Crocketts' house. He couldn't believe what had just happened. The Engbergs had a thief for a daughter, yet they were blaming him. He thought that he probably should have told them about the incident with Joel French's wallet. Maybe it would have made his own position less vulnerable. But then again, they probably wouldn't have believed him. And besides, it would have been betraying Brandy, and Gilberto couldn't do that.

* * *

Tuesday morning, the Crocketts took Maddie to Canyon High School to register. That morning at breakfast, Maddie had told Gilberto that she was going to try to get into Mr. Rhineman's class.

"Great," Gilberto said. "Maybe I'll see you there later."

When he got to drama class, Gilberto saw that Brandy wasn't there. But evidently she had talked to Ming the night before because Ming was telling Lee Wheeler what had happened at Putnam's.

"Oh, man," Lee said. "I'd hate to be

Brandy right now."

"Me too," Ming agreed. "Her parents are really coming down hard on her. They're acting like jailers. They grounded her and took away the keys to her car. Can you believe that? Brandy was crying so hard she could hardly talk to me."

"Poor Brandy," Gilberto said, joining them.

"Yeah, and she said they're not too crazy about you either," Ming said.

Gilberto nodded. "They yelled at me last night and blamed me for putting her up to stealing."

"They are so clueless," Ming said. She lowered her voice. "Brandy's been stealing things for years. I know because I've had to cover for her sometimes. I told her to stop several times, but she just doesn't seem to be able to."

"Gee, they're being awfully hard on her if they don't think it was her fault, aren't they?" Lee said.

Ming shrugged. "I guess they're just warning her to stay out of trouble."

Gilberto thought he knew why the Engbergs were being so hard on Brandy. It was their way of saying they didn't like her friends—namely him.

"I really feel sorry for her, Ming," Gilberto said. "I just can't turn away and forget about her."

"Gil, you'd *better* forget about her," Ming advised. "Her parents are big shots and can make trouble for you if they want. If they think you're leading their precious little daughter astray, they'll go after you with a vengeance."

"I don't know," Gilberto said, shaking his head. Then he remembered Maddie. "Say, I've got a friend who might be starting in this class today. Her name's Maddie. She's been through some pretty rough times. Could you, like, be friendly toward her? It would mean a lot to me."

"Sure," Lee said.

"No problem," Ming concurred.

A few minutes later, Mr. Rhineman appeared followed by Maddie. "Sorry I'm late, class," Mr. Rhineman said. "We've got a new student. This is Madeline."

Maddie quietly corrected him. "Maddie," she said.

"Sorry, Maddie," Mr. Rhineman smiled.

"Okay, now, if my memory serves me correctly, there's an empty desk in front of Gilberto. Right, Gil?"

"Yep," Gilberto said. "She can sit right here."

Maddie smiled and took the seat in front of Gilberto.

When class got underway, Lee and Ming went out of their way to make Maddie feel welcome. And when the rest of the class saw what Ming and Lee were doing, they followed suit. Gilberto was grateful to his friends for coming through like that. He had hoped that his friends would be Maddie's friends, but he wasn't sure that guys like Lee Wheeler would warm up to the skinny little girl with the big fawn eyes. For the first time in his life, Gilberto was finding out what friendship meant and how friends come through for you when you need them.

Gilberto could not get Brandy out of his mind all day. He kept thinking of all the great times they'd had at play rehearsal. And he remembered the kiss she had given him the night they went to the movies. He hated the thought of her sitting at home in her room feeling like a prisoner.

After school, Gilberto worked at Hamburger Haven where he was able to lose himself in the busy routine of making hamburgers and fries. About seven o'clock he was surprised to see Joel French enter the restaurant. He hadn't spoken to Joel since the billfold incident and still resented the treatment he had received. Since Gilberto was the only one at the counter, Joel had no choice but to go to his register.

Joel hesitated, obviously ill at ease, and then said, "A Big Burger and a large order of fries."

"Anything else?" Gilberto asked coldly.

"Yeah, a chocolate malt," Joel answered.

"For here or to go?" Gilberto asked.

"To go," Joel said.

Gilberto rang up the sale. "That'll be $5.23," he said. Joel handed him the money.

As Gilberto gathered up Joel's order and put it in a sack, he noticed that Joel kept glancing at him. When Gilberto handed him his food, Joel said, "Look, Gilberto, Lee told me about what happened with Brandy. I guess I owe you an apology for accusing you of stealing my wallet. Looks like it was Brandy that day."

Gilberto didn't like to hear Joel say that Brandy was a thief, even if she was. He considered lying and saying that he had stolen the wallet. But then he realized that covering up for Brandy, as Ming had done, was wrong. In fact, it had probably encouraged her stealing habit.

"It's all right," Gilberto said.

"Friends?" Joel asked, offering his hand.

"Friends," Gilberto said. The two boys shook hands.

"I just have to ask you one thing," Joel said. "Did you know that Brandy took my wallet?"

Gilberto nodded.

"Well, I admire you for not telling," Joel said. "It took some guts to do that."

Gilberto shrugged. "I'm glad I didn't," he said. "Brandy's got a problem, but she's basically a good person."

Joel nodded. "Well, you're not so bad

yourself," he said. "See you later."

Gilberto smiled as Joel left the restaurant with his sack. Looks like I've got another friend, he told himself.

Gilberto worked until ten o'clock and then headed home. He was amazed at how tired he felt and could hardly wait to get into bed. After telling Mr. and Mrs. Crockett goodnight, he headed upstairs to his bedroom.

When he passed Maddie's room, he saw that the light was still on. "'Night, Maddie," he whispered.

"'Night, Gil," Maddie said. "And thanks."

"For what?" Gilberto asked, standing outside the door.

"For helping me get here, to the Crocketts', I mean," Maddie said.

"You're welcome," Gil said. "I'm glad it worked out."

"Me too," Maddie said. "It's great here."

Gilberto chuckled. "Just wait until Wednesday nights when you have to eat Mrs. Crockett's liver and onions," he said.

From the other side of the door, he could hear Maddie giggle softly. It was the first time he had heard her laugh. He figured she was going to be okay now.

* * *

The next morning, Gilberto was heading toward the high school entrance when Mrs. Engberg pulled up in her royal blue Cadillac. With a sneer on her face, Brandy got out of the car. She was dressed in black jeans with holes in the knees, a black Metallica T-shirt, and black boots. Her eyes were lost in eye make up, and her hair was teased and snarly.

"I'll pick you up right here after school," Gilberto heard Mrs. Engberg say.

"Yes, Commandant!" Brandy snapped, saluting her mother briskly. She stomped away from the car and joined Ming, who happened to be standing nearby.

"Brandy, you look . . . different," Ming said.

Brandy laughed a short, caustic laugh. "She hates it when I wear this stuff," she said. "I told her that if she wants to kill my social life, then I'm going into mourning. I'm wearing black until I get all my stuff back."

She marched by Gilberto without even noticing him. As she passed, he heard her tell Ming, "Mom is going to regret the way she's treating me. She thinks she's got me right where she wants me, but she's wrong. Someday she's going to wish she'd treated me differently."

Gilberto was shocked by what he had seen and heard. She looked and acted like a different person. It was as if the light within Brandy had gone out, leaving only darkness.

10

In drama class, Gilberto looked for Brandy, but she didn't show. "Where's Brandy?" he asked Ming.

"In the counselor's office," Ming said. "Her parents are making her talk to a counselor before she goes back to class."

"Man, they're really serious about this, aren't they?" Lee asked.

"Well, they've got their name to consider," Ming said. "The Engbergs don't want their daughter tarnishing their reputation."

At lunch, Brandy found Gilberto and sat down beside him. "Oh, Gil," she groaned. "This is killing me!"

"It'll pass, Brandy," Gilberto said. "You'll get through it."

"They're blaming you for what I did, Gilberto," Brandy said. "It's just their way of keeping us apart."

"What you did?" Gilberto asked, shocked to hear Brandy admit to the crime.

"All right, all right," Brandy said. "I confess. I tried to steal the pants, but I couldn't help it. I just wanted them so bad.

Besides, what does it matter? Those clothes are probably made by poor kids in Taiwan who work for pennies an hour. Putnam's has no right to charge so much. In a way, it's their fault. I wouldn't have tried to steal the slacks if they wouldn't have cost so much."

Brandy must have seen the amazement in Gilberto's eyes. "Oh, don't look at me like that," she said. "Haven't you ever taken anything that didn't belong to you?"

"Actually, no," Gilberto said. "Well, maybe an apple from someone's tree or something like that."

Brandy said nothing.

"Did you tell your parents you tried to take the pants?" Gilberto asked.

"No," Brandy said. "I thought it would just make matters worse."

Gilberto was hurt. It bothered him that Brandy was willing to let her parents continue to place blame on him, but he didn't say anything.

"Anyway, they took my car keys, and I'm grounded," Brandy said. "I'm not allowed to do anything on the weekends."

"For how long?" Gilberto asked.

"Until I prove to them that I'm the nice, little girl I used to be—whatever that means. They expect me to jump through hoops like a trained seal. Get this—my mother put a chart on the wall, and every time I break one of the rules, I get a red *x*. Mom says I have to go for a full month without a single *x* before they'll even talk about giving me back my privileges."

"They'll probably feel bad and let you off the hook before then," Gilberto said.

Suddenly anger boiled over in Brandy's eyes. "Well, they'd better," she said. "Because I haven't done my homework yet this week—and I don't plan on doing it. Let's see how my parents like it when my grades drop."

"Brandy, that's just adding fuel to the fire," Gilberto said.

"I don't care," Brandy declared. Gilberto could see tears in her eyes. "If they're going to make my life miserable, then I'm not going to try to please them anymore. What more can they do? They've already taken away everything I care about."

With that, she got up and walked away.

* * *

The next day, Gilberto happened to be in front of Canyon High when Brandy's mother dropped her off again. As Brandy got out of the car, he could see that she looked pretty much the same as yesterday—dressed in black with outlandish make up and hair.

"Brandy," Gilberto heard Mrs. Engberg saying. "If we didn't love you, we wouldn't be doing these things. We're trying to help you grow up right."

"Love me?" Brandy shrieked. "You hate me! And I hate you!" She flung down her book bag, spilling books, pens, and paper all over the sidewalk. Then she started to stomp away.

Mrs. Engberg got out of the car. "Brandy! Come back here and pick that up!" she ordered.

"Pick it up yourself!" Brandy yelled over her shoulder.

Shaking her head, Mrs. Engberg stooped down and collected the contents of the book bag. Then she gave it to one of Brandy's friends to give to Brandy later.

* * *

During supper at the Crocketts' house that evening, the doorbell rang. Mr. Crockett went to the door, and soon agitated voices floated into the house. Within minutes, Mr. Crockett was leading Mr. and Mrs. Engberg into the dining room where the others sat. Mrs. Engberg glared at Gilberto and demanded, "Where is our daughter?"

Gilberto was shocked. "I saw Brandy at school today, but I haven't seen her since."

"How do I know I can believe you?" Mrs. Engberg said.

Mr. Engberg, his eyes full of anger, drew close to Gilberto. "We know the influence you have on our daughter, and we believe you know where she's gone."

"Wait a minute!" Mr. Crockett said with uncharacteristic authority. "You have no right to come into my home and accuse the people who live here of anything! Gilberto left for school and came home as usual. If he says he doesn't know where your daughter is, he means it. I've never known him to lie about anything."

"Our daughter has disappeared," Mrs. Engberg said, with just the slightest hint of shakiness in her voice. Gilberto could tell that she was struggling to keep her composure. "Apparently, she didn't attend any of her afternoon classes, and now she's gone. We've called all her friends. No one knows anything."

"Well, then, I think it's time you call the police," Mr. Crockett said matter-of-factly.

Gilberto stood up. "I don't know where Brandy is. Honest. She didn't say anything to me about leaving. But I care a lot about her. And I hope when you find her, you'll go a little easy on her. She's really mixed up right now."

Mr. Engberg gave Gilberto a withering look. "I don't think we need a lecture from the likes of *you*, young man."

"Mr. Engberg," Mr. Crockett said. "Your troubles with your daughter have nothing to do with *our* Gilberto. I'm respectfully asking you to leave our house *now*."

Indignant, the Engbergs left the house. Gilberto stared with amazement at Mr. Crockett. Had he really said *our* Gilberto?

Mr. Crockett had stood up for Gilberto as if he were his own son.

"Thanks, Mr. Crockett," Gilberto said softly.

"Well, right is right," Mr. Crockett said, rejoining the group at the table. "Now let's finish eating."

***

No one saw anything of Brandy for the next three days. A major storm system had moved into the area, bringing thunder and lightning and heavy rains. Gilberto worried about Brandy. In his mind, he could see her huddled in the corner of some dark, dirty alley, cold and in despair. Gilberto recalled her bitter threat, *Mom thinks she's got me right where she wants me, but she's wrong. Someday she's going to wish she'd treated me differently.*

Outside Gilberto's bedroom window, the trees swayed like reeds in the wind. Gilberto thought about Brandy and had a hard time sleeping. He wanted to talk to someone about his concerns, but the rest of the house was asleep.

Gilberto decided to go down to the kitchen and make himself some hot chocolate. He remembered his mother doing that for him, and it had always seemed to help him sleep. He pulled on a pair of sweatpants and a T-shirt and went downstairs.

Being as quiet as possible, Gilberto tiptoed around the kitchen gathering milk, cocoa, and sugar for his hot chocolate. He was just turning on the stove when he heard someone behind him. He turned to see Maddie standing in the doorway.

"Hi," she said, rubbing her eyes and yawning. "What are you doing?"

"Making some hot chocolate," Gilberto answered. "Want some?"

"Sure," Maddie said. She took a seat at the kitchen table.

"Did I wake you?" Gilberto asked as he added more ingredients to the kettle on the stove.

"No," Maddie said. "I was awake. In fact, I haven't been asleep yet."

"Something bothering you?" Gilberto asked.

Maddie shrugged. "I guess you could say that," she said. "It's got to do with my being on my own for so long."

Gilberto frowned. "What do you mean?"

"Well, in the last year," Maddie began, "there have been a lot of times when I've had to sleep in . . . dangerous places, I guess you'd call them. Alleys, phone booths, park benches. A lot of times I didn't sleep. I just lay there all night, afraid to close my eyes. I guess I got so used to being afraid of sleeping that now I have a hard time, even though I know I'm in a safe place. Every time I fall asleep, I wake up in a panic, afraid that there's danger lurking nearby. Sort of a survival instinct, I guess. Crazy, huh?"

Gilberto poured the steaming hot chocolate into two big mugs and took a place at the table across from Maddie. "I don't think so," he said, placing a mug in front of her. "I've never slept well either. Not since I started getting shuffled around from home to home. And I wasn't even in danger. But just the same, I never really felt safe either. So I think I can relate to what you're saying."

The two sat in silence, sipping the hot drink, when suddenly they heard a light knocking at the back door. Maddie looked at Gilberto in panic. He could tell she was genuinely afraid. "Relax," he said, patting her hand. "I'll see who it is."

Gilberto sounded more at ease than he felt. He glanced at the clock on the stove—after midnight. He wondered who would be knocking at the Crocketts' door so late at night.

When he reached the door, he pulled the curtain aside slightly. There on the porch, drenched and shivering, stood Brandy Engberg. Quickly, but as quietly as he could, Gilberto opened the door.

"Brandy!" he said. "You look terrible. Get in here."

"Th-th-thanks," Brandy stuttered.

"Maddie, can you get her something warm to put on?" Gilberto asked. "She's freezing."

"Sure," Maddie said. Immediately she disappeared up the staircase.

"Where have you been, Brandy?" Gilberto asked. "Everyone's been worried about you. Your parents were here looking for you."

Just then Maddie returned with a flannel shirt. "I'm Maddie," she said. "Here. Put this on."

She wrapped the shirt around Brandy's shoulders and went to the stove and poured the last of the hot chocolate into a cup. "Drink this," she said, placing it in front of Brandy. "It'll warm you up."

"Thanks," Brandy said. She grasped the mug in her cold hands and took a sip. Then she looked at Gilberto. "I've been hiding out in a motel downtown until I could decide what to do," she said. "They didn't care that I wasn't an adult, as long as I could pay."

She took another sip of hot chocolate. "Anyway, I've decided to leave town in the morning. I came to say good-bye because I care so much about you. Of all the things my parents took from me, taking your friendship was the worst."

"But why would you leave town, Brandy?" Gilberto asked. "Your parents are worried sick about you."

Brandy shook her head and said, "I doubt that. The way they've treated me lately proves that they're not too concerned about me."

"That's not true, Brandy," Gilberto said. "I know they've been rough on you, but they love you."

Suddenly Maddie spoke. "Where will you go?"

Brandy shrugged. "I'm just going to the bus station and buying a ticket to someplace that sounds exciting—Los Angeles, maybe, or New York. I thought maybe I could get a job as a waitress and work my way into modeling or something."

Maddie smiled. "I don't mean to be cruel, Brandy," she said, "but do you know what a waitressing job pays? Not enough to pay the rent, I can tell you that. I tried it."

"What do you mean?" Brandy asked. "You're saying you lived on your own?"

Maddie nodded. "For the last year," she said. "And it wasn't fun or glamorous or anything like that."

"What do you mean?" Brandy asked.

"After I ran away from home, I headed for the big city," Maddie said. "It didn't take long before I was doing drugs. Pushers prey on runaways. And let me tell you, they saw me coming—a small town girl from Connecticut. Anyway, pretty soon I was out of money. I got a job waitressing, but it wasn't enough to pay the bills, let alone pay for my drug habit. I lost my apartment and started living on the streets."

Brandy pulled the shirt tighter around her shoulders and stared in silence at Maddie.

"Then I got head lice," Maddie went on, "and had to eat out of restaurant dumpsters. The stale, spoiled food made me sick. One time I was sick for three days, but I didn't have enough money for medicine. Luckily I found a free clinic that helped me beat my habit. They called my parents, but before they could come get me, I took off again. That's when I headed west and ended up here in Springville. Now I realize how stupid I was, but it's too late. My parents don't even want me anymore."

"My parents don't want me either," Brandy said. "They hate me."

"That's what I thought," Maddie said. "My parents placed all kinds of restrictions on me and made up a bunch of new rules. They called it 'tough love,' only all I could see was the tough part. I didn't realize that parents could be that tough on their children because they loved them."

"How did you know they loved you?" Brandy asked.

"I found out they had spent tons of money looking for me the first few months," Maddie explained. "They put ads in newspapers and on the sides of semi-trucks. Whenever an unidentified girl's body was found, they'd go to the morgue, hoping it wasn't me. Do you know how hard on them that must have been?"

Brandy shook her head and bit her lip. "I can't imagine," she said.

"Anyway," Maddie said, "they gave up after I ran away from the clinic. When the Department of Human Services in Springville contacted them a few days ago, they said they didn't want me anymore."

"Would you go back if you could?" Brandy asked.

"In a minute," Maddie said.

Then Brandy started to cry. "But they've

been so mean to me," she sobbed. "I don't want to live with all those rules."

Maddie reached out, covered Brandy's hand, and said softly, "They're just trying to tell you that they care about what happens to you," she said. "That they want you to grow up to be a decent person. Don't you think they deserve another chance?"

For a few minutes, Brandy didn't answer. As the three sat in the warmth of the Crocketts' kitchen, the only sound that could be heard was Brandy's soft sobbing. Finally, Gilberto reached out and put his arm around her. "So can we take you home now?"

Brandy nodded and buried her face into his shoulder. "Go tell Mr. and Mrs. Crockett," Gilberto said to Maddie. "Explain what's going on and that we'd like to use the Volvo to take her home."

"Oh, Gilberto," Brandy said when Maddie was gone. "You're too good for me."

Gilberto chuckled. "That's the first time I've ever heard that," he said.

"You know about my stealing problem, and yet you still try to help me,"

Brandy said.

"Problems can be fixed," Gilberto said, "if you're willing to admit to them, that is."

"I am now," Brandy said, a small smile appearing on her face. "That's the first thing I'm going to talk to my parents about."

Gilberto looked into her eyes. Even wet and bedraggled, she appeared beautiful to him.

"Are we still friends?" Brandy asked.

"I was hoping we were more than friends," Gilberto said. He leaned over and kissed her lips softly.

Just then Maddie, dressed in jeans and a sweater, reappeared in the kitchen. "They said to be careful," she said as she handed Gilberto the car keys.

"I will," Gilberto said, leading the two girls out the door.

When they pulled into the driveway of Brandy's house, they noticed that the porch light was on. "They must have left it on for me," Brandy said. Gilberto thought he could hear relief in her voice that her parents still wanted her back.

The three walked to the door and rang

the doorbell. A few minutes later, Mrs. Engberg appeared with Mr. Engberg right behind her.

"Brandy!" they cried at the same time. Mrs. Engberg reached out and folded her daughter into her arms. Then she led Brandy inside, leaving Gilberto and Maddie on the porch. As they turned to go, the door reopened and Mr. Engberg rushed outside.

"Wait!" he cried. Gilberto and Maddie stopped. Mr. Engberg said in a trembling voice, "Brandy told us you talked her into coming home. Forgive us, please. We judged you too harshly."

Gilberto nodded and led Maddie to the Volvo. Mr. Engberg hurried back into the house.

Once inside the old car, Gilberto and Maddie grinned at one another, and their hands met in a high-five. "All right!" they sang out together and headed back to the Crocketts' house, the place they now called home.

Novels by Anne Schraff

PASSAGES

An Alien Spring
Bridge to the Moon
(Sequel to *Maitland's Kid*)
The Darkest Secret
Don't Blame the Children
The Ghost Boy
The Haunting of Hawthorne
Maitland's Kid
Please Don't Ask Me to Love You
The Power of the Rose
(Sequel to *The Haunting of Hawthorne*)
The Shadow Man
The Shining Mark
(Sequel to *When a Hero Dies*)
To Slay the Dragon
(Sequel to *Don't Blame the Children*)
A Song to Sing
Sparrow's Treasure
Summer of Shame
(Sequel to *An Alien Spring*)
The Vandal
When a Hero Dies

PASSAGES 2000

Just Another Name for Lonely
(Sequel to *Please Don't Ask Me to Love You*)
Memories Are Forever
The Hyena Laughs at Night
Gingerbread Heart
The Boy from Planet Nowhere